Showing More SYMPATHY

Learning to CARE

Jasmine Brooke

FOX EYE
PUBLISHING

Tiger sometimes was not **KIND**. She was often not **SYMPATHETIC**.

If her friends were **UPSET**, she did not always notice. If Tiger's friends **HURT** themselves, Tiger often walked away.

At school, Mrs Tree had asked everyone to bring in their favourite book, so they could share it with the class.

After the books had been read and shared, Mrs Tree asked everyone to find their book, so they could take it home again. But Zebra could not find her book. "Oh no!" she said. "It is my favourite book!"

Zebra was very SAD.
But Tiger just shrugged her shoulders and walked away.

At break time, everyone played outside. Tiger called to Wolf, "Come play with me!" Then she chased Wolf around the biggest tree.

Wolf ran and ran, having fun. But then he tripped and fell. "OUCH!" Wolf gasped. "My knee!"

At lunchtime, Cheetah smiled, "Ooh, chocolate cake – that's my favourite!" But there was only one piece left.

Now, Tiger liked chocolate cake too. She liked it very much. "Oh!" gasped Cheetah when Tiger took the cake. "There's none left for me."

Cheetah felt HURT.
But Tiger just walked away.

In the afternoon, everyone made paper hats, then played outside. "Look at me!" Gorilla called, wearing his hat. But then, a gust of wind lifted up the hat. It swirled up and up, and out of sight!

Gorilla was very UPSET.
But Tiger just walked away.

The next day, no one played with Tiger. At lunchtime, Cheetah took the last piece of cake. Then, in the art class, when Tiger lost her picture, everyone just shrugged their shoulders. They all looked away.

Tiger felt **UPSET**. She felt very **SAD**.

Her friends didn't CARE.
They were not KIND.

Mrs Tree knew Tiger had not meant any harm. "I can see you are **UPSET**," she said. "But if you show that you can be **KIND**, I think others will be **KINDER** to you, too."

Tiger thought about her friends and how **UPSET** they had been. She wished she had shown a little more **CARE**.

The next day, Tiger helped Zebra to find her book. When Bear hurt her arm, Tiger asked, "Are you OK?" At lunchtime, Tiger let Cheetah have the last piece of cake. She also helped Gorilla make another hat.

Tiger felt happy because **CARING** felt so good.

Tiger had learnt to be KIND and to show how much she cared.

Words and feelings

Tiger was not very kind in this story. She found it hard to show that she cared and that upset her friends.

CARING

HURT

There are a lot of words to do with being kind, showing sympathy and being unkind in this book. Can you remember all of them?

UPSET

SYMPATHETIC

KIND

Let's talk about behaviour

This series helps children to understand and manage difficult emotions and behaviours. The animal characters in the series have been created to show human behaviour that is often seen in young children, and which they may find difficult to manage.

Showing More Sympathy

The story in this book examines issues around not being kind. It looks at how not being considerate of others when they feel upset can make them feel sad. It also explores how friendships can be harmed when people do not act kindly.

The book is designed to show young children how they can manage their behaviour and learn to be sympathetic.

How to use this book

You can read this book with one child or a group of children. The book can be used to begin a discussion around complex behaviour such as being sympathetic.

The book is also a reading aid, with enlarged and repeated words to help children to develop their reading skills.

How to read the story

Before beginning the story, ensure that the children you are reading to are relaxed and focused.

Take time to look at the enlarged words and the illustrations, and discuss what this book might be about before reading the story.

New words can be tricky for young children to approach. Sounding them out first, slowly and repeatedly, can help children to learn the words and become familiar with them.

How to discuss the story

When you have finished reading the story, use these questions and discussion points to examine the theme of the story with children and explore the emotions and behaviours within it:
- What do you think the story was about? Have you been in a situation in which you were not kind or sympathetic? What was that situation? For example, did a friend feel upset but you did not show them sympathy? Encourage the children to talk about their experiences.
- Talk about ways that people can learn to be sympathetic. For example, think about how you would feel if you were upset and a friend was not kind to you. Talk to the children about what tools they think might work for them and why.
- Discuss what it is like when people are not kind. Explain that because Tiger was unsympathetic, her friends were upset and in turn, they were not kind to Tiger when she was upset.
- Talk about why it is important to be kind to others. Explain that by learning to be kind we make others feel better. When people are kind, others learn to be kind too. If everyone shows kindness to one another, everyone will feel happier and supported.

Titles in the series

 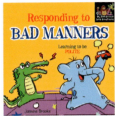  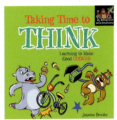 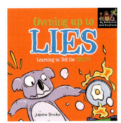
 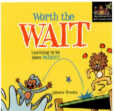 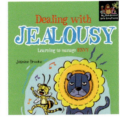 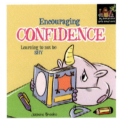 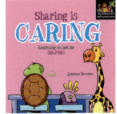
 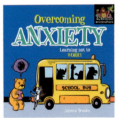 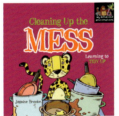 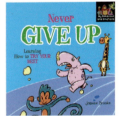 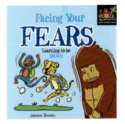
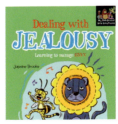  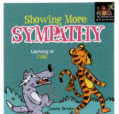  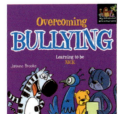

First published in 2023 by Fox Eye Publishing
Unit 31, Vulcan House Business Centre,
Vulcan Road, Leicester, LE5 3EF
www.foxeyepublishing.com

Copyright © 2023 Fox Eye Publishing
All rights reserved. No portion of this book may be reproduced in any form without permission from the publisher, except as permitted by U.K. copyright law.

Author: Jasmine Brooke
Art director: Paul Phillips
Cover designer: Emma Bailey & Salma Thadha
Editor: Jenny Rush

All illustrations by Novel

ISBN 978-1-80445-304-9

A catalogue record for this book is available from the British Library

Printed in China